When I Was Five

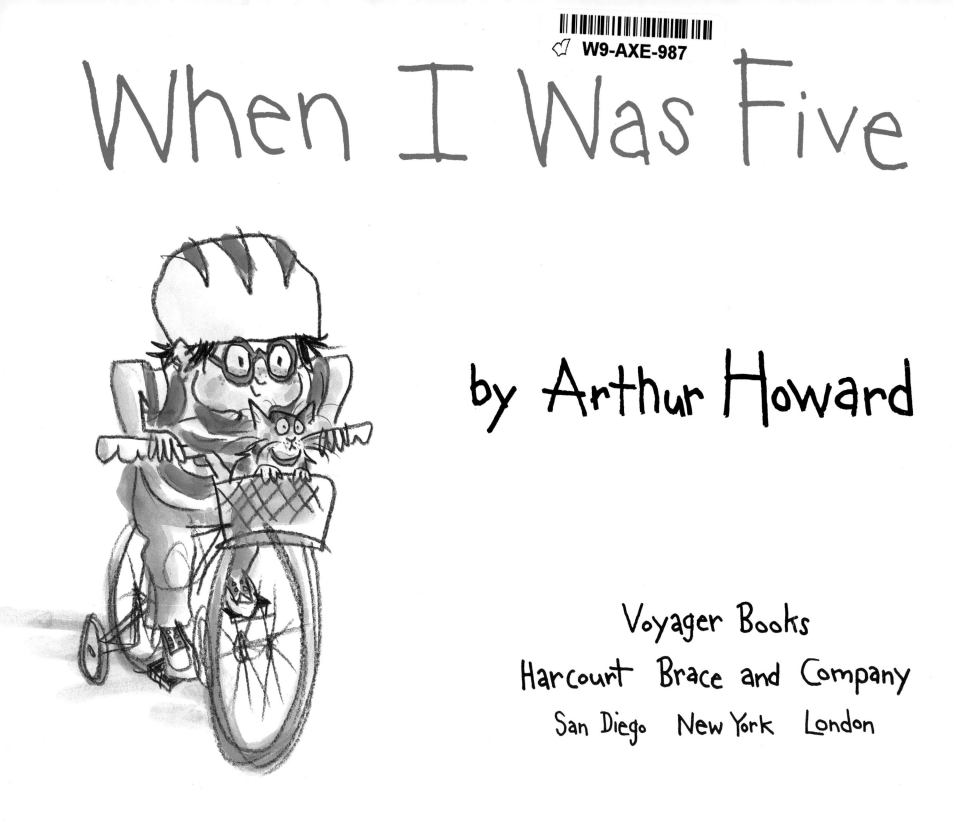

by Arthur Howard

Voyager Books
Harcourt Brace and Company
San Diego   New York   London

First Voyager Books edition 1999
Voyager Books is a registered trademark of Harcourt Brace & Company.

The Library of Congress has cataloged the hardcover edition as follows:
Howard, Arthur.
When I was five/Arthur Howard.—1st ed.
p. cm.
Summary: A six-year-old boy describes the things he liked when
he was five and compares them to the things he likes now.
ISBN 0-15-200261-8
ISBN 0-15-202099-3 pb
[1. Growth—Fiction.   2. Identity—Fiction.   3. Friendship—Fiction.]   I. Title.
PZ7.H8324Wh   1996
[E]—dc20   94-43987

E F

Printed in Singapore

The illustrations in this book were done in watercolor, gouache,
and black pencil on 90-lb. drawing paper.
The text type was hand-lettered by Arthur Howard.
Color separations by Bright Arts, Ltd., Singapore
Printed and bound by Tien Wah Press, Singapore
Production supervision by Stanley Redfern and Jane Van Gelder
Designed by Arthur Howard and Camilla Filancia

for Beverly

When I was five

I wanted to be an astronaut

or a cowboy

or both.

When I was five this was my favorite kind of car,

this was
my favorite
kind of dinosaur,

this was my favorite secret hiding place,

and this was my
best friend, Mark.

Mark
had
a
dog
named
Peggy,

a brother who used bad words,

and bunk beds—
my favorite
kind of bed
when I was five.

BABE RUTH

Cal RIPKEN Jr

and I want to be a

major-league baseball player

or a deep-sea diver.

Now that I'm six

this is my favorite kind of car,

this is my favorite
kind of dinosaur,

this is my second-best hiding place (my favorite one is a secret),

Some things never change.